MARVEL
SPIDER-MAN

MARVEL

Twin Tales

Two Great Stories... One Great Book!

MILES MORALES SPIDER-MAN

AUTUMN
PUBLISHING

AUTUMN
PUBLISHING

Published in 2022
First published in the UK by Autumn Publishing
An imprint of Igloo Books Ltd
Cottage Farm, NN6 0BJ, UK
Owned by Bonnier Books
Sveavägen 56, Stockholm, Sweden
www.igloobooks.com

@ 2022 MARVEL

MARVEL

Designed by Steve Prosser
Edited by Alexandra Chapman

0622 001
2 4 6 8 10 9 7 5 3 1
ISBN 978-1-80022-324-0

Printed and manufactured in China

This book belongs to:

....

THE AMAZING SPIDER-MAN

Peter Parker was just an ordinary kid, until a school trip to a science fair led to him being bitten by a radioactive spider.

The bite gave Peter super strength and the amazing ability to cling to walls - just like a man-sized spider. So Peter Parker decided to become a Super Hero called Spider-Man!

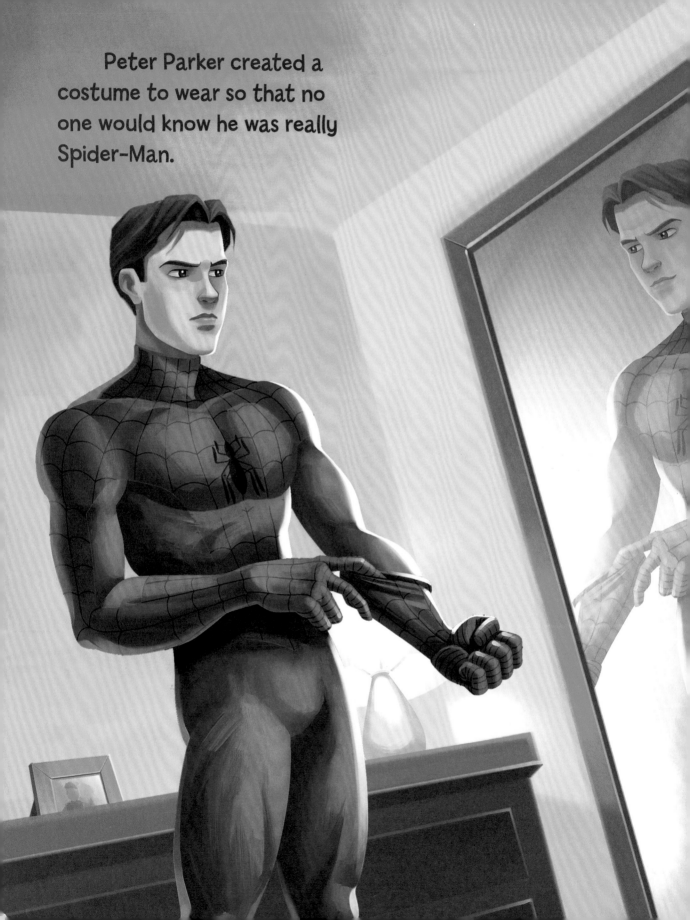

Peter Parker created a
costume to wear so that no
one would know he was really
Spider-Man.

Peter also invented web-shooters that allowed him to swing through the city from building to building.

He can make a shield for protection...

... or a parachute to float safely to the ground.

And Spider-Man can use his webs
to stop bad guys in their tracks!

Spider-Man also has a "spider-sense", which alerts him to danger. When his spidey-sense starts tingling, Spider-Man knows there is trouble nearby!

Some people, such as J. Jonah Jameson,
publisher of the newspaper *The Daily Bugle*,
think Spider-Man is a menace. They don't trust
him because he wears a mask to hide his face.

But most people know that Spider-Man is really a hero!

No trouble is too big - or too small - for Spider-Man to handle!

MEOW!

He always enjoys helping out - even if there is no crime to speak of!

Because he fights bad guys,
Spider-Man has made lots of enemies.
Super villains are always looking for a
way to get rid of the Wall-Crawler!

The Vulture
wears a winged
costume that doubles
his strength and gives him
the ability to fly. Whenever
this bad bird soars into town, he
causes trouble for Spider-Man!

Doctor Octopus is armed and dangerous! His four metal tentacles are strong enough to lift lorries as if they are toys. "Doc Ock" would like nothing better than to squash Spider-Man like a bug!

The Sandman is made of living sand! He can slip through the smallest cracks or make his fist rock-hard to smash his enemies. But Spider-Man thinks fast and always cleans the floor with this gritty thug!

The Lizard was once a doctor - but his research with lizards turned him into a half-man, half-reptile monster. Spider-Man needs all his amazing powers to escape the Lizard's whipping tail and sharp claws!

HISSS!

The Green Goblin commits crimes with a rocket-powered glider and a bag full of explosive pumpkin bombs. The Goblin's gloves can fire powerful electric shocks, so Spider-Man has to move fast when he faces this frightful fiend!

The world is a much safer place because Spidey keeps on swinging. Go, Spider-Man!

I'm Miles Morales. I used to have a normal, ordinary life. I lived with my family. I went to school. And I did a lot of homework.

That was until I was bitten by a weird spider!

WHAAA!

I passed out - and when I woke
up, I could STICK TO WALLS! Crazy!

I could make amazing leaps!

I could turn invisible!

With just a touch of my hand, I could
deliver a shocking venom strike!

BREAKING NEWS-BREAKING

Q Dat

Somehow, that spider bite
had given me amazing powers,
just like the original Spider-Man!

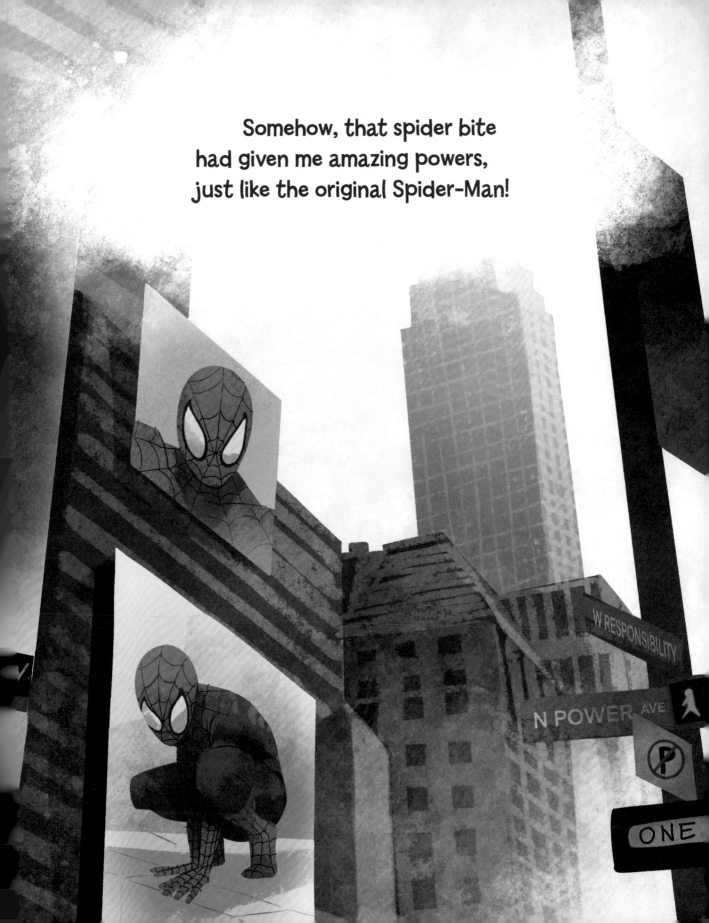

I began to realise that the world was starting to need heroes more and more.

There seemed to be new super villains and monsters popping up every day!

At first, I didn't want to be a Super Hero. I wasn't even sure I could *be* a Super Hero.

But when you have the power to help people, you just have to find it within yourself to do it!

With great power comes great responsibility, so I made the choice: I chose to be a hero!

My best friend, Ganke, is the only person who knows my secret. He even helped me with my first costume.

... as well as some
real villains, like Electro.

It wasn't long before I came to the attention of
Nick Fury. He is the leader of S.H.I.E.L.D., which is sort
of a police force that protects our entire world.

He gave me this new outfit - with web-shooters.

Being the new Spider-Man is awesome!

I'm making friends. And I think
I'm getting the hang of being
a hero...

... but there's nothing easy about saving the world on a school night!